little senses

This Beach Is Loud!

by Samantha Cotterill

I CAN DO IT!		
Read about beaches		⭐
Play barefoot in sandbox		⭐
Try on and pick swimsuit		⭐
Pack for the beach		⭐
⭐ ⭐ ⭐ ⭐ = BEACH DAY!		

Dial Books for Young Readers

For Carter

Dial Books for Young Readers
An imprint of Penguin Random House LLC, New York

Text and illustrations copyright © 2019 by Samantha Cotterill

Visit us online at Penguinrandomhouse.com

ISBN 9780525553458
Special Markets ISBN: 9780593111789 Not for resale
Printed in China
1 3 5 7 9 10 8 6 4 2

Design by Mina Chung • Text set in Futura and Cooper Std
This art was created with ink, charcoal, and block print on watercolor paper.

This Imagination Library edition is published by Penguin Young Readers, a division of Penguin Random House, exclusively for Dolly Parton's Imagination Library, a not-for-profit program designed to inspire a love of reading and learning, sponsored in part by The Dollywood Foundation. Penguin's trade editions of this work are available wherever books are sold.

Beach Day!

**Let's go,
let's go!**

**I made
you breakfast,**

did *all* the packing . . .

. . . and even got
myself dressed.

...s and some insects live in sand? Turtle...
...ne world is in Brazil. Can we go there...
...ry. I really can't eat them. I think th...
...t's 9:55. How many more minutes da...
...be there at 9:58? Dad! I need to pee! D...
...to Brazil? D... knocked my wate...
...wet! DA... 9:59. Dad? D...
...dehydra...

Beach Day!

This beach looks ... busy ...

Let's try
over there . . .

How much
longer?

Sharkie is
heavier than
he looks.

There's sand in my boots!

I don't like sand.

Now it's in my suit . . .

. . . AND ON SHARKIE!

HOT! HOT!

YOUCH!

Daddy, I don't like the beach and I want to go home. The sand is **ouchy** and sticky and and bumpy scratchy... and Sharkie doesn't feel the same and and ...

Take a deep breath and give Sharkie a squeeze. Now tap your fingers and count to three . . .

I'll set up your fort while you choose a drink from the cooler.

Hmm . . . it needs something.

Maybe this flag?

And Sharkie wants a moat.

squeak
squeak...

dip
dip...

splish
splosh...

Splash!

CRRRRASH!!!

pat
pat

stomp
stomp

scoop
scoop

Dad! Dad! DAD! When can we go back? What time can we come back tonight? Where are the it's 6:00 pm. I'm hungry. Where that th crackers I love? Did you know that the seagull can drink both fresh an salt wate l need to pee